THINGS IN THE WOODS

Terrifying True Stories

Volume 1

ERIK LAKE

FREE REIGN

ISBN 13: 978-1-953462-87-9

Free Reign Publishing, LLC
San Diego, CA

Contents

Introduction

The woods have always held a certain kind of magic. Whether you've felt it while sitting alone in a clearing surrounded by towering trees, or in the quiet whisper of the wind rustling through leaves, there's an undeniable presence that the wilderness holds. But magic, as we know, can be both wondrous and dangerous, comforting and chilling, and this book—*Things in the Woods*—delves into the latter with unnerving precision.

Our ancient ancestors knew well the duality of the forest. It was both a place of resources and a realm of the unknown, where gods and spirits were believed to dwell. It is a landscape where the line between the ordinary and the extraordinary becomes increasingly blurred, and that ineffable feeling that you're not alone grows stronger with each step deeper into its belly.

In this anthology, you'll find a curated collection of true stories that shed light on the more terrifying aspects of the woods—accounts that defy logical explanation and scientific rationale. Here, the focus isn't just on the physical predators that roam the forest, but also on the spectral entities and inexplicable phenomena that many have claimed to encounter. From tales of Bigfoot and Sasquatch sightings, to stories about the inexplicable lights and haunting apparitions, to first-person accounts of eerie sounds and disquieting occurrences, this book aims to offer a comprehensive look into the shadowy corners of our woodlands.

These are stories that tap into our most primal fears, challenging our perceptions of the natural world and forcing us to question what could be lurking just beyond the boundary of what we can see and understand. As you delve into these pages, you may find yourself gripped by a sense of curiosity, or perhaps a lingering skepticism. Whatever your disposition, it's important to remember that for every story included here, there are likely many more that remain untold— kept secret due to fear, disbelief, or the understandable worry that nobody would accept such an outlandish tale as truth.

So we invite you to step beyond the tree line, into a world that exists at the edge of human understanding.

Turn on your flashlight, keep your senses alert, and whatever you do—don't wander too far from the path.

Because in the woods, you're never truly alone. And as you'll soon discover, that's a thought both fascinating and terrifying in equal measure.

Welcome to *Things in the Woods*.

- Erik Lake

Chapter 1
BIGFOOT

IT WAS the summer of 2015 and a few of my gal pals and I went on a camping trip to Yellowstone National Park. Every year we would go somewhere and just enjoy and renew our friendship. This trip seemed a little out of character, a little bit more outdoorsy than normal, but I was up for it. We set up our camp in a rather secluded area. It was surrounded by huge trees and a dry lake over to the other side of us. In the distance, I could see a few RVs, but we were the only open tent campers in that area.

Our first night in Yellowstone was wonderful. It was uneventful. There were soothing sounds of nature that lulled us to sleep. I began to think that maybe I could do this camping thing and that it was not so hard. However, around 3AM, I was rudely awakened by a peculiar and unsettling noise. It was a series of bizarre sounds like someone standing outside of my tent and screaming out "whoop whoop whoop". I peeked out the opening of my tent. I could see my friend's tents close by, but there was nothing else around us. Whatever was making the sounds had to have been in the woods.

As my senses sharpened, I realized that the strange calls were being answered in the distance, as if some unseen creatures were communicating through the night. The air was still. There was a very foul odor hanging around our tents. It smelled like someone with incredibly bad body odor had been in our camp, except it was much worse.

I was still looking out the opening of my tent. It was beautiful outside with a partial moon. My eyes adjusted and I was able to see better in the darkness. While I was looking out of the tent, I heard what sounded like a large tree branch crashing to the ground. It broke the silence with a deafening crack. I was waiting for my friends to come flying out of their tents, but apparently, they slept through it. I went back inside and crawled into my sleeping bag. I was able to fall back asleep directly. My mind was still racing with explanations of what that sound might have been.

The night got quiet again and I was almost asleep.

Just as I was drifting out of consciousness, there was another loud bang that echoed through the night. It was loud and close, and my heart began beating incredibly fast. The noise was so loud, it sounded like it was in our camp.

My friends had still not emerged from their tents. I was beginning to think they could sleep through anything. but instantly, I heard a deep, bone-chilling roar that echoed through the night and the valley. It was extremely loud and intense. It was probably 200 yards away from us. but it was deep in the woods. I instantly thought that it was a bear or some other wildlife. I could tell by the intensity of the volume; this creature was large.

As if that were not enough, I suddenly heard two high-pitched screams. That was enough to wake my friends, and they came bolting out of their tents in a panic. Jane, one of my friends, whispered that she could smell something putrid, like rotting trash. I couldn't help but wonder if some bear had ravaged a nearby trash pile, but the smell was fleeting and faded into the night after a few moments.

Now that the three of us were awake, we had a moment to chat. We decided to all move into one tent for safety. I had the largest tint of the three, so together we all huddled our sleeping bags together and tried to go back to sleep. I listened to the unsettling noises in the distance. fear finally had gripped us all and we were unable to fall back asleep. It wasn't long before dawn, so we opted to get up and make a fantastic breakfast to make up for the lack of sleep.

When we emerged from the tent, I was expecting to find the campground in disarray, evidence of some nocturnal visitor's rampage. Much to my surprise, everything appeared exactly as it had the day before. There were no signs of trash thrown all around, there were no disturbances in the surroundings. it was as though the unsettling events of the night left no phys-ical trace on this earth.

We decided to make the best of our day, and we continued to explore the park. We hiked throughout the day on and off. On our way back to camp, we stopped at the campground store. As I was checking out, I couldn't help but resist mentioning the strange things that had been happening the night before to the clerk who was on duty. I asked if she had ever heard of people reporting such things.

She gently smiled as she bagged our items. She did reveal that there had been several reports, sightings, and strange occurrences that have been happening. The employees were given instructions not to talk about it to tourists, but since we were a group of three women alone, she felt we should know. She revealed that over several months there had been many reports and occurrences that were related to sasquatch. With more and more tourists visiting the park, the sightings had apparently been on the rise. She said most Park officials do not acknowledge them because they do not want to scare away the tourists. She slipped something into our bag at the end of our transaction. I saw her do it but I did not know what it was. When I got the bag and started to leave, I looked inside. There is a can of bear repellent. I looked at her and smiled and mouthed the words "thank you". She smiled and nodded.

Even though I understood what she was saying, I was still in disbelief. I was trying to wrap my head around the possibility that what we heard might have been sasquatch. I had mixed emotions about it. I was both thrilled and excited, yet I was also frightened and terrified.

My friends were outside in oversized wooden chairs waiting for me. I caught up with them, but I chose not to tell them about the possible Sasquatch activity in the area. While we were not overly girly girls, we were still not the rough and rugged Outdoors people like so many people here. I thought that information was best kept on a need-to-know basis, and they did not need to know.

That night was surprisingly peaceful. There were no sounds like the night before that had haunted us. The woods were still except for the normal sounds of the nocturnal life that lived in the woods. I could hear small animals walking around, birds singing, and the occasional sound of a bat taking flight overhead. We were able to finally get some rest, but we all stayed in one tent again. For the rest of the night, we did not hear anything. We were able to enjoy our last night at Yellowstone. It was extremely peaceful and a fantastic way to end our trip. The next day we packed up our supplies, went on one last short hike, and then left. I always wondered if we had encountered Sasquatch that first night.

Chapter 2
HORNED CREATURES

GROWING up in a rural pocket of Pennsylvania, my childhood was a collection of classic Americana memories, especially the idyllic summers on our family farm. Yet, what sticks out the most are not the typical hayrides, sweet corn, or even the magnificent fireflies that came alive at twilight. No, what haunts me to this day is a series of inexplicable, unsettling encounters with otherworldly beings I can neither identify nor forget.

The first time I crossed paths with these entities, I was just ten, recently recovered from a bout of a nasty stomach flu. My body clock was entirely off-kilter, sleep eluding me on that fateful night. My bedroom was spacious, designed to accommodate myself and my two older sisters, both of whom were sound asleep. Not wanting to disturb them, I quietly made my way to a cushioned alcove that housed a large, picturesque window overlooking our farm and the adjacent woodlands.

Clutching my favorite novel and a flashlight, I settled down. That night, the moon was a radiant sphere, filling the room with an almost supernatural luminosity, rendering my flashlight unnecessary. I tried to immerse myself in the book, but kept catching fleeting movements in my peripheral vision. When I looked, nothing seemed amiss, and I blamed it on lingering illness or perhaps a trick of the light. Finally, my curiosity overpowered me; I focused my gaze intently on the spot near the tree line where I thought I'd seen something stir.

It took only a few minutes for a sense of palpable dread to sink into my bones. My skin prickled as if stung by a hundred nettles. The alcove, my haven of tranquility, now felt like a cage. And then I saw them—four grotesque beings, standing in a tight cluster near the woods. They were impossibly tall, maybe twelve to fifteen feet, their bodies elongated and skeletal, as if constructed from rubber. Their anatomy defied all earthly logic; their torsos were almost concave, an eerie hollow where their stomachs should be.

In the moonlight, their forms cast sinister silhouettes. It was difficult to see facial features, but they appeared to have the basic structure of eyes, noses, and mouths. What arrested my attention were the horns— each creature possessed them, thick and formidable, each unique in its curvature and spiral, terminating in what seemed like a vicious point.

In that paralyzing moment, they seemed engrossed in some sort of conversation, gesturing towards the treetops with their abnormally long, sinewy arms. Then, as if sensing my presence, all four twisted their heads in unison and stared directly at me. Their faces, previously unclear, seemed twisted in sadistic glee. The air grew heavy, almost suffocating. Terrified, I bolted for my bed, cocooned myself in my quilt, and prayed for morning.

The next day, my father casually mentioned something that turned my blood cold. Birds, nests, even owls —everything that lived in the trees had been massacred, blood drained, bodies scattered under the very trees the creatures had been near. I kept silent, knowing my stoic father wouldn't tolerate tales of nocturnal monsters.

Over the years, I've had numerous encounters with these inexplicable beings, each time chipping away at my skepticism and fortifying my fear. The episode that remains most vivid happened when I was around 17, during an isolated afternoon fishing trip at a stream on our property. It was the eerie silence that initially unnerved me; no birds sang, no rustling leaves, just a deafening quiet. And then, as if summoned by my apprehension, they appeared again, only this time in full daylight. Their faces were the stuff of nightmares, mouths filled with serrated teeth, their eyes demonic—crimson with black flecks, almost glowing from their sunken sockets.

I fled, and they chased. As I dashed through the forest, they materialized alongside me, their bodies warping like those inflatable "wacky waving tube men" you see at car sales events, always watching me.

Even now, years later and residing in a different state, I sense them. They are closing in, and my deepest fear is that someday, my own children or grandchildren might find one lurking under their bed or hiding in their closet. What they want or why they have fixated on me, I can't say. All I can do is hope time will bring answers—or at least, an end to these haunting visions.

Chapter 3
SHADOW ENTITIES

I NEVER THOUGHT in a million years that I would be someone who would have a paranormal encounter to write about. Don't get me wrong, I've always believed in the paranormal, Halloween has always been my favorite holiday and I love horror movies just as much as the rest of my family, which is a lot, but I thought that if I hadn't experienced anything by the time I was twenty-eight years old then I probably wouldn't, and I came to terms with it. I come from a family who constantly talks about how plagued they are with all sorts of paranormal phenomena but it just hasn't ever happened to me. That is until I had a child. I was twenty-eight years old. I had been married to the love of my life for three years at the time and we had been together for five and we were ready. The only issue we had was where we were living at the time. We rented a little one-bedroom house in the middle of a very high crime community. We had both delayed college a little bit and were grad students and honestly that's all that we could afford. My grandmother, bless her heart, made us the offer of a lifetime and we honestly had no choice but to take it. We didn't care though and would've jumped at it anyway. My grandparents owned a lot of real estate throughout the county we lived in but once my grandfather passed away ten years earlier she was having a hard time handling tenants and started selling off all the homes and properties one by one and little by little. The only properties she kept were her own home and the summer lake house. The summer house was where the whole family got together in the summer so that we could spend time with grandma and, to spend time in the woods and at the lake. Some of the best memories I had as a kid and growing up were at that lake house. My grandmother said she would let us pay her a low rent, something extremely affordable, until we eventually paid the house off. We all knew that she probably wouldn't be alive once it was all paid off, just because of how long it was going to take, how old she already was and how her health had been declining at that time, so she put a clause in the contract that once she passed it would be ours free and clear, along with all the property attached to it. Most of my family didn't exactly rejoice at the idea but my grandmother knew my husband and I were trying our very best and knew that we couldn't raise a child in the area where we were living. It was such an incredible offer and we started making plans to move right away.

To get to the point of this story, I'll have to fast forward about five years, to when my son was five. He had always been afraid of his bedroom in the house from the time he was in a crib and couldn't do anything but cry but that was when he was finally able to and ready to articulate exactly what the issues were. He would scream in the middle of the night and come running from his bedroom into mine and my husband's and no matter how we tried to calm him down or convince him he was only having bad dreams, he could not be convinced or consoled but as I said, it was nothing new. However, once he had to start school, we knew the summer before that we had to do something so one night in the middle of July, after an entire month and a half of failed attempts to get him to stay an entire night in his room, my husband and I had enough. We let him stay with us that night but the following morning we insisted he tell us what was going on. We would see bruises and scratches on his body and he would say things like that he was seeing the shadow man with the red eyes peeking out from his closet door even though we knew we had closed it. He said the shadow beings would come up from under his bed and grab him and hit him while he slept and all sorts of other strange things. The scariest for me was when he told us that the night before the hat man with the red eyes, who normally hung out in the background, watching while the other shadow people attacked him, crept out of his closet and stood by the door to his room, telling him that he was only a quick run away from the freedom of the hallways and that he better decide soon if it would be worth trying to get past him to get there. This all sounded incredibly evil and demonic to me and once he started talking he didn't stop for a while. I was devastated because I believed him right away and knew there was nothing he could have been watching on the television that would have given him this terrifying information or wild story in his head. It had to have been real.

My husband however is a total nonbeliever. Well, he was at that time anyway, and he yelled at our son and told him that he wasn't allowed in our room anymore and that he needed to be a big boy and stop making up horror stories because he was going to scare me, his mom. My son's face immediately dropped and he didn't even argue or try to defend himself. He simply said that he would stop and walked away with his head down. That night, to make him feel better and much to the annoyance of my husband, I told my son that I would sleep in his room with him, in the chair, so that I could see what was going on for myself. He was so relieved my heart broke and I kept my promise. Nothing happened even though I begged whatever evil was lurking in there to show itself to me and to leave my son alone. For a whole month my son had no issues and was able to sleep through the night without anyone in his room and without waking up looking like he had just been beaten up and terrified. My husband was sure it was his tough love tactics but I wasn't and I had a feeling of dread that was almost overwhelming me. I wasn't comfortable leaving my son in the room anymore but to keep the peace I didn't say anything. I simply pretended to use the bathroom and would creep down to his room at night and peer through the door to make sure nothing was going on and I had been doing that for the entirety of the time that he was at peace in there. I somehow knew it was only a matter of time before it started up again but I had no way of knowing just how bad it would end up being.

I was on the phone with my mother and I had explained everything to her and when I told her my feelings about what was going on and why it had suddenly stopped, she told me I should call one of my cousins who I hadn't talked to in a while. There was no reason we hadn't spoken, just that life happened and we lost touch for a few years. I asked her why but she told me just to do it and so I did. I couldn't believe it when my cousin told me that she had the same exact experiences when staying in that room during her visits to grandma's summer house all throughout her childhood. I asked her why she never said anything and she said she was told not to tell any of the other kids because it would scare them. I then found out that out of seven cousins, I was only one of two who had never had any sort of paranormal experiences there. I asked her what she thought the reasons were and she said it was simple. Myself and the second to youngest cousin, who was the other one who hadn't seen anything, weren't involved in a Ouija board session that was held one night when it all began. We had been sleeping in the living room with our parents instead of in that bedroom with all the other kids. They had summoned something and all of them have since been haunted by the same types of things my son had been experiencing since he was a baby. I called my other cousins and they all admitted it and backed her up, some of them rather reluctantly. I was devastated and tried to talk to my husband about it but he wouldn't listen. He accused me of making it worse by feeding into our son's "fantasies" and I knew then it would be me who would have to make sure we got rid of whatever was there. I waited until last weekend before he would be starting school, when my husband and his brother were taking my son camping near his brother's house, and that's when I did what I thought I needed to do.

I saged the whole house and said suggested prayers the whole while. However, the house didn't feel lighter at all when I was done and my son's room specifically felt even more overwhelming. I decided to sleep in there and try the Ouija board myself. I knew it was in the basement because it was there when we moved in but I never gave it a second thought and had planned on getting rid of it anyway. I went into my son's room and tried to use the board but for a whole hour nothing happened. I knew something had been in there with me the whole time though, it just wasn't answering me. I was planning on sleeping in his room and just as I was turning out the lights and getting into bed I just happened to glance out of his bedroom window and I saw a black shadow person with red eyes staring up at me from one of the trees that surrounded the backyard.

I was terrified instantly but ran outside anyway. I was hell bent on confronting whatever it was. I brought the sage with me and said all the suggested prayers again and I was in those woods for a good hour as well, trying to sage away the evil that was obviously coming out of the woods and into my home, into my son's bedroom. I'm trying to make this long story short so I was attacked in his room that night. I was dragged out of bed and slammed onto the hardwood floors of the cabin. The hat man with the red eyes crept out of the closet and walked past me to the front door. Five or six other shadow people held me down while the hat man taunted me and asked me if I thought that I could get past him and make it to the door. The air was thick with evil and I couldn't move or scream. I woke up on the floor and immediately called my grandmother. After explaining everything to her that had been happening in the house, she gave me a number of a friend of hers who she claimed specialized in things like what I was dealing with. The woman came right over and we walked through the woods. After we were done she did some sort of ritual that she said would seal the evil in the woods but that I would have to upkeep all of it monthly for as long as we lived there. She explained that there had always been something evil living in the woods and that the hat man is just one of the many forms it can take on to terrorize people, especially kids. She said some are more open than others and that's why I never saw anything but my son was so affected by it. She taught me how to do the protections and keep it at bay and that's what I did, the whole time my husband and I looked for another place to live. My son was never terrorized by shadow entities or any other paranormal creature ever again.

There were several times when I would be outside in my backyard at night when I would see the red eyes peering at me out of the dark but I tried my best to ignore it. We couldn't go to the lake anymore or on walks through the woods because I had trapped the evil in there and it wanted nothing more than to get its "hands" on me. I knew that without a doubt, if we went into those woods, or swam in that lake, we would live to regret it. My husband didn't understand it and the whole ordeal was so traumatic it ended up affecting our marriage and we divorced two years later. My son has since been able to see paranormal entities both good and bad ever since but he has worked hard to be able to keep it under control and from controlling him. I left out a lot in this story and tried to make it as short and to the point as possible. Don't play with Ouija boards and especially not when surrounded by woods where you have no idea what's lurking and just waiting to have an opening to attack and feed off humans. They will always choose the most innocent souls to go after and most of the time, that's our children. Thanks for letting me share.

Chapter 4
HUMANOID CREATURE

THE SUMMER NIGHTS were always full of magic when we went camping as a family. But that night in 2006 changed everything. Everything about camping as a child always seemed full of magic. I think that's the way of being a child. But magic can be terrifying, especially when it stares you right in the face. We were nestled deep in the pine forests of Alden, Iowa at Wildwood Campground, our home away from home. The familiar musty scent of our little log cabin greeted us once again. As soon as Dad's old station wagon came to a stop, I burst through the door, ready to explore. As I had many times before. I even got first pick of the beds. My dad ran his fingers through my hair as I rushed to load things into the cabin. It was always his silent way of saying, 'I love you."

Twelve years old and hungry for adventure, I couldn't wait to hit the trails. My younger brother Ronny, on the other hand, dragged his feet as he sulked about missing his video games and friends. At only eight years old, the thought of fishing all day or gathering around a campfire at night wasn't nearly as exciting to him as it was to me. He wanted to stay in video game land and avoid the rest of us like the plague. But I wasn't going to miss a single moment.

After a long day of trekking through the misty woods, we returned to our cozy cabin. It looked like something plucked straight from a fairy tale, with its rustic pointed roof and round windows. As the sun began to set, shadows crept across the walls inside. The wind blustered up the wind making tap, tap, tap noises against the window and roof. I chose the small back bedroom and its lumpy futon bed, while Ronny collapsed onto the sofa, whipping out his GameBoy. My father came in and stroked his hand through my hair before heading back outside into the porch.

"Time for bed soon!" Mom called. But Ronny was too engrossed in Pokémon to listen. I snuggled under a quilt, comforted by the gentle wind whispering through the pines outside. This was the best white noise ever. My heavy eyelids closed as I dreamed of the adventures the next day would bring. Sometime later, I awoke to an eerie sensation of icy fingers stroking my hair. Confused in my groggy state, I leaned into the familiar touch, assuming Dad was saying goodnight. But when I reached to pat his hand, my heart seized in my chest. Instead of Dad's soft warm skin, I felt something slippery, cold and... scaled? I whipped my head around to see a most horrific sight.

As I opened my eyes, I saw a humanoid creature crouched next to me, so close I could smell its fetid breath. The moonlight filtering in through the window illuminated its grotesque features. It had an unnaturally long face, made even more terrifying by the row of sharp, needle-like teeth jutting from its lipless mouth. Its skin resembled that of a salamander - slick, moist, and pale gray in color. But most disturbing of all were its eyes. Bulging and crimson red, they seemed to glow with menace in the darkness. Those sinister eyes bored into mine, devoid of compassion or humanity. I saw its fingers on its other hand tapping against the hard wood.

The creature's elongated fingers continued to stroke through my hair, its slimy claws leaving trails of filth. Its scent was like damp, rich soil. As it leaned closer, its rancid earthy smell overwhelmed me. I tried to scream, but sheer dread silenced my voice. The creature widened its cavernous maw, revealing a throat as black as a bottomless pit. Was it planning to swallow me whole?

Just then, the bedroom door crashed open, and blessed light flooded in. The creature recoiled and vanished before my eyes. But the image remained seared into my mind - Its eerie glowing eyes. The needle teeth poised to shred flesh. And the foul, earthen smell of the thing that didn't seem to belong in our world. Mom rushed to my side; her face etched with worry. "What happened, sweetie?" I sat bolt upright, heart hammering, eyes darting wildly around the empty room. Dad's strong hand stroked my hair. "Did you have a bad dream?" I knew what I saw! I shuddered when she ran her fingers through my hair. Thinking of those salamander-like fingers sliding their way over my scalp, embracing the loose tendrils made me want to wretch.

I could barely choke out a whisper. "I saw...I saw something. Red eyes. Sharp teeth. It was here..."

Dad tried to soothe me, assuring me they had been right outside on the porch and would have noticed anything amiss. Mom glanced nervously out into the darkness and suggested perhaps a frightening shadow had sparked my imagination. But I knew what I saw. And what I felt - those icy claws raking through my hair. It was no mere figment of my imagination.

Despite their comforting words, I knew there would be no more sleep for me that night. I clutched my quilt tight as Dad tucked me in, double-checked my nightlight, and planted a kiss on my head. As they left the room, I glanced anxiously around. Just shadows and silent furniture now. But the disturbing image of that creature remained seared into my mind. I prayed for sunrise, wondering if the light of day would make the darkness of night feel like a distant dream. But deep down, I knew this lurking terror was now a part of me. And the woods of Alden would never feel quite as safe or magical again.

Chapter 5
MEADOW SIREN

GROWING UP, I rarely ventured into the meadows. In the heart of Wyoming, meadows stretched for miles, kissing the horizon with their gentle slopes and soft tufts of grass. My home was nestled on the edge of the largest meadow, the Elmsworth Meadow. My family relished outdoor excursions – picnicking, playing, and laying beneath the sky – but from my earliest memories, the vast openness of the meadows unnerved me. Despite my reservations, each summer, my parents signed me up for the Meadowland Camp two towns away.

The camp was my yearly dread. Open skies with unending stretches of green, kids I didn't recognize, and games I loathed. Due to our financial struggles, benevolent folks from our community would sponsor my and my cousin's stay for the entire summer season. But the summer of 1989 held a twist. To bolster my college application, I got the chance to intern as a junior instructor at the camp. Figuring it'd be better to lead than follow, I accepted, my tuition generously covered by our kind neighbors.

I reached a week before the camp's official start for preliminary instructor training. The first month was rigorous, preparing us for our roles, but it gave me the choice of domain – and I chose the lakeside activities. Our accommodations were quaint tents, with junior instructors like me separated from our mentors by a mere patch of land. On the night my life changed forever, only three of my fellow trainees had arrived, with others scheduled to join later.

Taking advantage of our extended curfew till midnight (unlike the 10 pm one for the kids), a fellow intern named Ethan asked if I fancied a stroll across the meadows. His secret stash of contraband cigars was incentive enough. Though I never smoked, the idea of sharing a clandestine moment appealed to me.

We ventured deeper into the meadows, ensuring we were well away from prying eyes and noses. A small clearing surrounded by wildflowers seemed perfect. Lighting up, we chatted about college plans and our crushes from previous camp years. But our light banter was interrupted by an eerie hum emanating from a thicket nearby.

Curiosity piqued, we approached the source. Our single torchlight revealed nothing. But the humming, growing louder, led us further into the meadow, each step taking us farther from familiar grounds. The vastness around felt ominous, and the once comforting glow of our campfire was a mere speck in the distance.

Suddenly, behind a rise, the humming morphed into an unsettling song. Mustering courage, we decided to confront the source, thinking it might be some campers pulling a prank. But what we saw was beyond comprehension. A luminous being, standing almost 8 feet tall, its skin shimmering under the moonlight. Its ruby-red eyes pierced the darkness, and it wore a mane of silver. Its slender body seemed to float, and the eerie song continued, sending chills down our spine.

Frozen in place, we watched as it tilted its head, seemingly sensing something. With lightning speed, it darted towards the distant lake, leaving a trail of luminescence. The splash that followed signaled its dive into the watery depths. Our legs found their strength, and we sprinted back to camp, not daring to look back.

Back in our tent, Ethan and I debated our next steps. Our experience sounded fantastical, and there was the risk of ridicule. We settled on silence, unless others mentioned similar sightings. The rest of the summer passed without incident, though the haunting song would sometimes drift into our ears on particularly quiet nights. My stint at the camp ended that year, and despite offers and parental pressure, I never returned.

Decades later, the memory remains vivid. Ethan and I, now connected through technology, often reminisce about that night. While we've found no concrete answers, our research hints at ancient legends speaking of "Meadow Sirens" – ethereal beings guarding sacred lands. Whether myth or reality, our encounter remains a testament to the mysteries the world holds, sometimes in the most unexpected places.

Chapter 6
BIGFOOT

IN 2022, I settled near Pine Peak, Colorado. My job with a regional woodworking agency involved crafting innovative homes. Some weekends, my friends and I would dive into the Rocky Mountain Reserve to escape the grind. This region, pristine and untouched, was our preferred spot for hiking and fishing trips. Given its wild character, we never forgot to carry our firearms.

After an especially hectic summer, we planned a lengthier escape to the woods. Joining the excursion were my friends, Sam, Dylan, and Alex. They made it to the campsite before me and set up my tent. As a gesture of gratitude, I was responsible for collecting refreshments. By the time I arrived, the trio was already relaxing by a freshly lit campfire.

The evening was perfect, filled with laughter and

stories, until around 11 PM when mysterious sounds broke the silence. The ruckus, coming from about 50 yards away, sounded like two massive creatures clashing. Aware that bears often roamed these terrains, we were on high alert.

Though Alex mentioned he'd seen trees marked with claws earlier, he believed it wasn't recent activity. Nevertheless, our firearms were within arm's reach. As the unsettling noises continued, we tried illuminating the source with our flashlights, but the dense woods revealed nothing.

An hour of wary vigilance passed before we decided to retire, ensuring our firearms were easily accessible.

The following day, as we drove to a neighboring lake in Sam's truck, we encountered a foul odor. Along the way, several saplings appeared damaged, snapped around 8 to 10 feet high, which was peculiar given no recent stormy weather.

Post a fulfilling fishing session, as evening approached and cloud cover intensified, the unsettling stench returned. Soon after, uncanny noises echoed again. They started like coyote calls but morphed into something more haunting, as though being imitated by a larger entity.

Around 9 PM, weariness overcame me and I

decided to rest. But sleep was short-lived. At 2 AM, terrifying screams and rhythmic knocking disrupted the silence. Emerging from my tent, I saw something that left me frozen: a silhouette, much larger than any human, standing at the forest's edge, its eyes reflecting the campfire's glow.

Dylan, who was also awakened by the noise, whispered, "Is that...Bigfoot?" The colossal figure stood there, observing us, its posture neither aggressive nor entirely passive.

After what felt like hours but was merely minutes, the creature retreated silently into the forest's depths. By morning, we found massive footprints around our campsite. Their human-like but oversized nature left little to the imagination.

Though we had initially planned a longer stay, the encounter made us unanimously decide to pack up and leave. The Rockies, we realized, held secrets more profound than we'd ever imagined.

Chapter 7
GHOUL

BACK IN MY cringeworthy goth phase as a teenager, I was so desperate to impress my crush Fen that I went along with his idea for all of us to hang out at the old, abandoned graveyard on the edge of town one night. Looking back now, I shudder at the reckless things I did to try and fit in with that crowd. But at the time, all I could think about was getting Fen to notice me. So, I raided my closet for the most outrageous goth outfit I could put together and coated my face in pale foundation and dark eyeliner.

When we got to the graveyard, some kids had set up a little makeshift party area with a boombox. As we cracked open some beers, I tried my best to act casual and cool, like hanging out in a graveyard at night was no big deal. Somebody put on "Bela Lugosi's Dead" and I started dancing in what I thought was a sexy, gothic way. Inside though, I felt ridiculous and awkward. Fen barely glanced at me as he laughed and joked with his friends.

Feeling dejected, I wandered away from the group to an old, broken tombstone shaped like a cross. I laid back onto the worn, cracked marble slab, trying to look mysterious and brooding. As I gazed up at the starry sky, I started hearing odd scraping noises in the distance. Trying to seem brave and impress Fen, I began loudly singing a creepy rendition of "The Unquiet Grave," a gloomy old folk song I thought fit the mood. The scraping sounds steadily drew nearer, even as I sang louder. Suddenly they halted, very close behind me. My heart froze, but I kept warbling in a quavering voice.

As I sang out into the night, the scraping sounds grew louder, until they suddenly stopped close behind me. Before I could react, hot, wet drops splattered across my face. Opening my eyes, I found myself staring up into a face from my worst nightmares. The ghoul was crouched atop the broken tombstone, so close I could smell its rancid stench - a mix of rotting flesh and stale earth from the grave. By the moon's dim light, I could see every grotesque detail.

Its skin looked decayed and leathery, clinging tightly

to its skeletal face. Patches were missing in places, revealing wet red muscle and sinew beneath. The skin surrounding its milky eyes sagged deeply. Dark blood congealed in the deep creases. It opened its mouth to unleash an unearthly moan, revealing jagged, broken yellow teeth coated in grime and old blood. Strings of saliva dripped from its cracked lips onto my face. I wanted to scream but could only shudder helplessly beneath its hulking body.

The ghoul's skeletal hands reached towards me, talon-like nails scraping the tombstone near my head. I cringed at the stomach-turning texture - rough and brittle like old chalk against a blackboard. Its grip was shockingly powerful when it grabbed a handful of my hair, yanking upwards. I shrieked in pain and terror, inhaling its choking decay smell. My scalp burned as I kicked and thrashed, desperate to break free. With a feral snarl, the ghoul bent its face toward mine, so close I was enveloped in its hot, damp breath. I gagged and squeezed my eyes shut, bracing myself for those jagged teeth tearing into my flesh.

I screamed in raw terror as its milky eyes fixed hungrily upon me. Scrambling to my feet, I turned and fled as the creature let out an unearthly wail. My friends froze in alarm around the boombox as I sprinted towards them. But before anyone could react,

Fen emitted a high-pitched shriek and took off running. One by one, the rest of my friends bolted after him, leaving me behind with the monster bearing down on me.

Summoning every ounce of adrenaline in my body, I raced blindly through the maze of graves and toppled headstones until I reached the dirt parking lot. I dove into my car, locking the doors right before the ghoul came crawling out of the darkness towards me. My heart pounded as I frantically turned the key in the ignition. I could see my friends' taillights disappearing down the road. Peeling out in a blind panic, I drove after them, praying the creature wasn't pursuing me. After putting some distance between me and the grave-yard, I pulled over to the side of the road, gasping and shaking. It slowly sank in how close I'd come to real danger and even death in that graveyard tonight.

I also realized with sinking disappointment that Fen wasn't the brave, take-charge guy I'd imagined. When things got scary, he'd taken off without a second thought, leaving me behind to save himself. In that moment, I decided I was done trying to reinvent myself to impress a guy. I wiped off the ghoulish makeup and changed out of that ridiculous outfit as soon as I got home.

I never went to that graveyard again, eventually

finding friends who appreciated me for me. These days, I look back on that era with embarrassment, grateful I outgrew chasing danger and bad boys. I learned to stop letting crushes and peer pressure lead me into perilous situations far too late. But at least I made it out of that nightmarish encounter in one piece to become a wiser person.

Chapter 8
UNKNOWN CRYPTID

I NEVER EXPECTED to get trapped outside in the woods, in the middle of a dense and very rugged forest, out in the middle of nowhere in Alaska where I lived at the time in the mid nineteen eighties, but that's exactly what happened to me. I was born and raised in Alaska and thought that I knew those same woods, that same forest, like the back of my hands. However, what was even more terrifying and fascinating was what I encountered while I was out there. I was in my thirties at the time and it wasn't abnormal for me to go camping deep in the forest in the middle of winter. You see, I was a part of a club that existed back then that for the time was unusual. Nowadays you will see thousands of clubs with people in it whose sole purpose of participating is to prove the existence of bigfoot but back then it was unheard of. Even the people like me who were doing it would keep it secret from their friends and even sometimes their close family members for fear of being thought to be crazy and losing their credibility both personally and professionally. I had an encounter with bigfoot when I was thirteen years old in that same forest and ever since I had been going once or twice a season, as many times as I could get away and do it really, to try and find proof of its existence. When it had first happened, everyone told me I was crazy and that it must have been a bear but I obviously knew by that age the difference between a bear and a bigfoot, but because of the way I was looked at and treated, even by my own siblings and parents, I eventually stopped talking about it and decided to go about my own quest to find it. Once I got married and bought my own home, I did so right on the outskirts of that forest and I hoped all the time that a bigfoot would just come stumbling out of the forest and onto my property. But nothing is ever that simple, and it turned out I would get much more than I was bargaining for when I went out there for the last time. The weather was supposed to be cold but mildly so, at least for the area, and I told my wife I just needed to get away for a weekend. She never questioned me. She was aware of the encounter I had years earlier and while she didn't know if she believed in bigfoot or not, she knew she believed in me, or so she said, and so when I wanted to sneak off into the woods on my own for weekend at a time occasionally, I was able to do so with no questions asked.

It wasn't supposed to snow and the first night I was out there I had no inkling at all that it would. My house was several miles into the woods from where I was camping but instead of driving around the forest and having to hide my vehicle to stay out there for a week-end, I just traversed through from my backyard. It was arduous and cold but I knew that if I could prove the existence of bigfoot or at the very least get some good evidence just to show all the people in my own family who had doubted me, it would have been worth it all. However, that didn't mean I was willing to die for it and at around one in the morning on the first night I was there, when the first flurries started to fall, I knew I was in trouble. I figured I would have to go back home and try again in a few weeks but I had no way of knowing how bad the weather was going to get overnight. I couldn't travel through those woods in the middle of the night, carrying all my gear and possibly coming up against wild and very predatory animals with nothing more than my camera and flashlight as weapons. I was worried but not overly so and knew the sun would eventually rise and I could pack up and head out. I was prepared for extremely cold weather and kept my fire going when I went to bed and let it put itself out. We weren't as careful back then with things like that, unfortunately. When I woke up at six in the morning I knew something was wrong immediately because the rising of the sun was being blocked out by what looked like a thick, large blanket covering my tent. It was snow, and there was about a foot of it on the ground and it was falling faster than I had ever imagined it could in such a short period of time. It had only been about five hours since I had seen the first flurries of it. I tried not to panic and decided to leave my tent and some other things I didn't desperately need while I walked back to my house. It was going to take me several hours and the conditions were nearly white out and I had to keep my wits about me if I wanted to get back in one piece. I obviously didn't have a GPS device or a cell phone so I also knew that if I wasn't home by the time it got dark outside my wife would have a search party out there, if she could gather one, because of the extreme and inclement weather that had come about so suddenly.

I bundled myself up and grabbed everything I needed in my backpack. I started walking in the direction of my house but I knew it was useless from the moment I took my first steps because of the conditions. I couldn't see an inch in front of my face and within seconds my nose was burning. I decided to do what I could to try and start another fire, and luckily I was always prepared for some snow or rain and had a few supplies that would help me do just that. However, before I turned around to go back to my tent and get started, I saw some strange footprints in the snow leading away from my camp. It was odd because they seemed to have just started out of nowhere, in front of a large tree stump. The stump looked like it had somehow escaped the brunt of the blizzard which was very strange indeed. It had a light dusting of snow all over it whereas everything else around me, other trees included, were absolutely and totally covered with the stuff. The footprints looked like a man's footprints but much larger and much wider and I thought immediately that they could very well belong to bigfoot. I headed in the direction they were traveling, following them, figuring I wouldn't be led too far astray because I was trying to keep in mind that if I got lost I was a dead man. The massive footprints went on for a while and while I was being mindful of not traveling too far away from my tent and camp, it was impossible to keep track and to keep that on my mind every second because of how anxious and excited I was. I thought that I had finally found what I had been looking for all those years. Eventually the footprints ended the same way they started, at a random, very large tree stump with the stump looking like it had been untouched by the several feet of snow that had fallen in such a short time. The forest was silent and I looked around hopelessly, realizing there was no way to find my way back to my tent and camp. My footprints were rapidly being covered up by the snow. It didn't make sense that the tracks remained so fresh up to the point of the tree stump because that would have had to have meant that whatever was leaving them behind was right in front of me the whole time. I would have heard something there even though I couldn't see it at all, or so I thought, and surely it would have noticed me following it and confronted me or something.

I took a folded tarp out of my backpack and several items needed to build a fire and that's what I did. It took a ton of effort to keep the fire lit and I was really scared I was going to freeze to death out there. Luckily I was well prepared and since I was so tired from all the walking and tracking the animal, whatever it had been that had left those tracks, I was able to nap for a few hours. When I woke up the sun was going down and the forest was eerily silent. I had propped myself up against that same tree stump that had been almost unbothered by the weather and I immediately noticed that something else was out there with me. I heard heavy breathing and what sounded like something trying to be quiet as it loudly took deep breaths and tried not to growl, which it was doing but very low and like it was trying not to. Whatever was out there knew I was there and was intelligent enough to try to not be caught or seen by me. In fact, once a minute or two had passed of me just sitting there and listening, all sounds ceased and the forest was completely and totally quiet again. The snow was still coming down and my fire had gone out long ago. I lit another one, just big enough to keep me and my area warm as I waited for the sun to set and hoped that whoever my wife sent out there to look for me would find me soon. I listened for any signs or sounds of like as the sun set. As I did so, I fell asleep again. The stress of the situation must have been making my adrenaline spike and therefore exhausting me without even having to do anything to cause it. I woke up and the sun was down. I was starving and so I had a snack and finished up the water in my thermos and filled it with snow just in case I would need it eventually.

I had to use the bathroom after chugging the water and so I got up to go and do so. It was such terrible conditions out there that I didn't dare stray too far from my makeshift camp and counted the steps in my flashlight as I went. I did my business and I heard a very loud crashing sound, as though a big tree had fallen somewhere around where I was. It scared me because what if one fell on me? When I turned back around and started following my footsteps, I kept my large flashlight trained at the ground on my prints the whole way. I made it right back to my little camp but immediately saw that something was wrong. My light hit the tree stump and it was turned over onto its side. I knew it was the noise I heard and I immediately walked towards it not only to inspect what had happened but to try and salvage my dry blankets and tarp so that I didn't get hypothermia from having to use wet bedding and whatever else. I walked right up to it and right before I was about to shine my flashlight in the hole underneath it, two eyes popped out and looked at me. I was terrified and I stumbled backwards and fell on my behind and into the snow. I kept my light trained on whatever it was as it crawled out of the hole underneath the large stump and I couldn't believe what I was seeing. It looked exactly like what we know as bigfoot but it was all in shadow. It was a shadow bigfoot! It dawned on me that if it could blend in with the shadows of the night, then perhaps it had a way to make itself invisible and that's how I wasn't able to see or detect it as it walked in front of me earlier in the day. Now, I didn't know this back then, but there are people who claim that bigfoot fears human beings because they see us as their biggest threat and they've developed a way to vibrate at a different frequency than us, in a matter of split seconds, to make themselves invisible to the naked human eye. That's not to say that animals can't see them or sense them and that's more than likely a good explanation for why everything in the forest that should have been there seemed to not be. The creature lumbered towards me and towered over me. It had giant yellow eyes and the exact shape of a bigfoot creature, standing at around thirteen feet tall and so very wide. I was shaking and it was evident by the flashlight moving around in my hand whereas earlier it had been so steady despite the freezing cold temperatures. I bent down and leaned in towards me and growled right in my face. I knew right then I had made a mistake as it seemed pissed off and its breath smelled so disgusting it's not ever something I could describe, and I've tried in my head so many times.

Within seconds of the creature leaning in and growling at me, it looked up and its shadow ears perked up as though it sensed or heard something. Then it grunted at me as it turned and made its way back down into the underground lair or whatever it was that was under that giant stump. I heard loud voices calling out for me and saw lights in the distance, followed by the sounds of snow mobiles. I screamed and eventually, within minutes, I was found and rescued. I immediately went back home but knew better than to tell anyone what I had witnessed and simply said I had walked off to the bathroom and couldn't find my way back due to the intense and heavy snowfall. I planned on going back when the snow started to melt to find my tent and other items left behind and to of course open those stumps up. I waited for the sprint to come and it was very hard. For weeks I stared out my back window and into my backyard, thinking the creature I had come across out there would have retained my scent and found me again but it never did and probably was completely uninterested in me and other humans in general if we stayed away from their areas. I was never able to find those trunks again. I found several that I thought could have been them but they weren't hollow and when I pried them up there were no holes or anything like that underneath them. I've often wondered if they had a way to do that too. Like, do they use illusion and things like that on us humans because we don't use all our brains and our senses aren't as fine-tuned as theirs are? I think that's the case but of course, I'll probably never know for sure. I still go out every once in a while and look for bigfoot and I've added some other cryptids to that list that are said to have been sighted around where I live and particularly in that forest but I've never had another encounter. Thanks for letting me share and when I get some time I'll write about the first time I saw bigfoot when it was in its regular skin and not a shadow. Though that time was a lot less terrifying.

PUBLISHER'S EXCERPT
MYSTERIES IN THE DARK: VOLUME 1

SWAMP THING

It took me a long time to come to terms with what happened to me and that's not because I had a hard time believing it, personally, because I was there, and I know what I saw. However, no one else ever believed me and most people I talked about it in the beginning made me feel like I was insane or needed some sort of mental help. It wasn't cool to have encounters like this back in the nineties, and it wasn't until the internet became somewhat what it is today that I finally became comfortable sharing my story again. I grew up hanging out in the woods near my house and all over my town, just like any other kid in rural Louisiana at that time. I was a little bit different though from my peers and neighbors in that I had always had paranormal experiences. Granted my parents and the other adults in my life chalked them up to nothing more than my overactive imagination but it was just something I sort of learned to deal with and keep to myself. I would often camp out in the woods at night and my parents never had a problem with it and most often they didn't even know where I was. Because of how I was raised and the things I had seen for as long as I can remember, I was an outcast. Not only that but I became a lot more spiritually aware then most kids my age. I was twelve at the time and this encounter is what eventually turned me into a religious man later in life. I just cannot put a name on what it was that I saw except to say that it was pure evil and ancient.

There were a lot of urban legends in the town I

grew up in and most of us kids did what we could to debunk them. In fact, I was only five years old when I had my first experience with what I believe was a demonic entity and it was while taking a dare for five dollars to spend two hours in the middle of the night and in the dark, in an old, abandoned house in the middle of the woods. My friends had parents like I had, for the most part, and so we were basically free to roam around all hours of the night and had no one looking after us. One night, after a particularly bad fight with my father, I stormed out of the house and was determined to get revenge by staying out in the woods all night long. I was too afraid to go back to the haunted house where I saw the demonic entity, but I knew the woods near it and surrounding the property were dense and dark enough that no one would be able to find me there. I ran out of the house, crying, and made my way over to the woods. There were woods everywhere in the town, but they were sporadically placed and only connected to homes periodically, all except for this one abandoned house. I got there and didn't have anything to sleep in or on or to keep myself warm or light my way. I considered going into the house, but it was warm enough outside and I figured if I really had to, like if anyone came looking for me, I could always change my mind and make my way inside of it. I found an old piece of cardboard in a dumpster in the backyard of the abandoned home, and I carried it into the woods with me. I was going to use it as a makeshift bed that night. I set it up but couldn't sleep. I thought the movement in the forest and the noises all the animals in the woods and the nearby swamp were making would keep me awake but it turns out there was nothing but silence that night. That was highly unusual and scared me almost enough for me to reconsider my terrible choice and go home for the night. Almost.

It struck me as so odd that everything was so still and quiet and made me so incredibly uncomfortable that I decided to walk around. I wanted to not only clear my mind and blow off some steam, but I also wanted to tire myself out. I walked and walked until eventually I came to the swamp. I didn't go right up to it but the sounds of the frogs and other animals in there were helping me to relax and I decided to curl up under a tree and lay down right there for the night. I hadn't brought the cardboard on the walk with me but didn't think it mattered as by that point it was already one in the morning and I was emotional and exhausted. The walk had worked along with the argument and other events of the day, to help me find a way to get to sleep. I was out before I could even give it a second thought. I woke up with a start to a loud and scary sound coming from the swamp. I couldn't tell if it was coming from around the swamp or inside of it but either way it was terrifying. It sounded like a giant, gurgling frog was somewhere there. I tried to shake it off as a regular and totally normal animal or amphibian and got up to use the bathroom. To do that, I turned my back on the swamp altogether. As soon as I was done doing what I had to do, I heard a loud splashing sound and then loud gurgling coming from a few feet behind me, right where the swamp was. I was already thinking that it was another ghost or other paranormal entity, and I wasn't looking forward to turning around to face it. I learned with goats and other paranormal entities that if you just ignored them and turned your back on them once you saw them, they would leave you alone and more than likely they would disappear altogether. That was my plan, but it didn't work out that way for me. I turned to face the horror I somehow knew was standing behind me.

It almost looked like a man at first. I didn't have a flashlight with me, but the moon and stars gave me enough light that I could make out the shape of it and most of the rest of it. It was around eight feet tall and muscular. It wore what looked like a man's wrestling suit with the shorts and the tank top/muscle strap things at the shoulders. It had a bare belly and chest and nothing on its arms or legs below the shorts. It looked like the material of your average wetsuit. The "man" stood awkwardly on two legs and his skin looked greenish and scaly. I noticed the tip of its tail waving back and forth behind it. I wouldn't say that the tail was wagging though because it was moving slowly back and forth. The tail was bright green like the scales on the rest of the man's body. I keep referring to it as a man because it also had a beard, which was green, of all colors and bushy green eyebrows. It had no eyelashes as far as I could see and its gigantic eyes that were much too large for its face were also bright green but with a vertical slit in them. The color of the slit in the eyes was reddish orange and not black like I for whatever reason had expected it to be. It gurgled loudly and moaned pitifully as black slime and sludge came pouring out of its mouth. It just stared at me the whole time, unblinking. The creature then turned and jumped into the swamp with a loud splash. I ran as fast as I could back to my house and that was the end of that. I tried telling my parents, my friends and even my siblings but no one believed me, so I was determined to probe them all wrong. After I was done being grounded for running away, I went back out there. I am leaving out details here that aren't pertinent to the story, just so you know. I decided that I was going to take pictures of the creature and I had my tent and flashlight with me and was more prepared that second time. I got into my tent but I aimed my flashlight at the swamp and set it up so it shouldn't have fallen. I had a brand-new roll of film in my camera, which was within arm's reach. I didn't mean to fall asleep, but I did eventually.

I woke up to the sound of my dad angrily shouting my name. I knew that wasn't possible or at least that it wasn't probable because a month had passed by, we hadn't had a fight and he was the one who gave me permission to go and camp in the woods. I got out of my tent anyway though and called back out to him. He told me to get my butt over to him immediately and that I was in big trouble. It was his voice alright and so I hustled my butt off to try and make it to him as fast as I possibly could. The whole time I was too distracted by what I could have possibly done wrong to think of the creature/man or much of anything else. I left behind the camera. Eventually it came time for me to walk past the swamp. I immediately saw all different colored small orbs of light and stopped in awe to watch them. They danced right before my eyes for about five minutes before blinking back out again one by one. The sound of my father calling me and sounding angrier than ever snapped me out of it. It sounded close but I couldn't tell which direction it was coming from. I turned to walk away but before I could yell out and ask him where he was, something grabbed my ankle and started pulling me towards the swamp. I was terrified and screamed bloody murder for my father and for general help. I turned and looked at what was dragging me as I tried and struggled to get away from it and get it to release me and I saw a green and scaly human hand wrapped around my ankle. It was strong, whatever it was but I managed to use my flashlight, which was heavy, to smash into it until finally it let me go. I got up and ran to a nearby tree, but I couldn't move too quickly because of how sore my ankle was. I looked back and saw the green man/creature coming out of the swamp. It slithered out on its stomach and when it looked at me and flicked its tongue out it was forked, like a snake or other reptiles would be.

Its arms were down at its sides while it slithered my way, but it opened its mouth and looked like it was grinning as I heard my father's voice yelling for me, coming out of the creature. I was so confused, and the terror was unlike anything I had ever felt or experienced before in my life. Suddenly and all in one quick movement it stood up. It stood there, just staring at me, and emanating a very aggressive energy. I tried to run home as fast as I could, but my ankle seemed to have been sprained or something. I made it out though, but I had left all my stuff behind and got grounded again and was forbidden from going into the woods anymore for a long time. I didn't argue with my parents on that one and in fact I decided right then and there I never wanted to go into those woods, or anywhere near that swamp and whatever else was lurking out there, ever again. My ankle was just severely bruised both on the inside and outside of it, so I guess I got lucky in that it didn't manage to drag me down into the swamp with it to do only God knows what with me and that my ankle wasn't permanently damaged. I didn't even bother to tell my parents or anyone else what happened to me because of what had happened the first time when I tried to tell everyone, which is what got me into trouble in the first place the second time. That's all for this encounter but I will be writing about the demonic entity in the haunted house as well. Thanks for letting me share and finally get this out there.

MYSTERIES IN THE DARK, VOLUME 1

Chapter 9
BIGFOOT

IN THE SPRING OF 2008, my wife and I built our dream home near the California / Oregon border. We could see Mount Shasta from our backyard. I had always heard about the crazy things that allegedly happened near there, but I never believed them. However, that summer, we had our fair share of experiences. One happened late in the summer.

I went to bed around 10 PM. It was not uncommon for my wife to stay up late watching TV or sewing in her craft room. One night my wife Martha was up late sewing. It was a nice evening and she had one of the windows open. She always enjoyed getting the evening breeze. This window overlooked Mount Shasta.

Martha was sewing away the night. She said the first thing she noticed was an odd smell that came drifting in from the backyard. She really did not want to close the window, but she could not take the smell anymore. she got up to go and close it, and that is when she started hearing the sounds. She said there were a series of wood knocks that were going on. While they were not directly in our backyard, our yard did back up to a wilderness area. I am assuming that is where the sounds were coming from.

While she was trying to figure out what kind of animal was making those sounds, she started to hear what sounded like a woman crying and screaming in the woods. There were blood-curdling screams that grew in intensity. Each one was more chilling than the last one. There was a scream that sounded like it was coming from our backyard, which frightened Martha and she ran into the bedroom to wake me up.

She asked me if I heard them. I was not sure what she was talking about. We have well-insulated windows, so I was not hearing anything that was happening outside. She told me to walk over to her sewing room. There were no lights on in the house and there were no lights outside. We could move with ease and go unde-tected if there was indeed something in our backyard watching us.

We carefully walked down the hall. I narrowly avoided a collision with a credenza but navigated around it and walked into her sewing room. The window was still open, and the air was different here. it smelled very foul. it was not the sweet-smelling air that we were used to. This was very rancid and reminded me of living back in the city.

I began to hear the shrieks that she was talking about. The quality of the screams was unlike anything I'd ever heard before. it seemed to oscillate between human and beast, landing somewhere in the middle. I was partially curious and terrified at the same time. If there was something in our yard making those screams, we did not want to be seen. We crouched down beneath her window and just listened. We positioned ourselves at the window, peering into the inky blackness that blanketed our yard and the road beyond. Once more, the haunting screams pierced the night. Whatever was producing that stench was getting closer to our home. It sounded like it was walking up and down the road, I could hear heavy footsteps on the gravel. it wandered with an unsettling persistence. The stench would get stronger as the cries got louder, but when the cries became further away I noticed that the smell was also trailing away.

Martha wanted to call 911, but I did not even know how to report this. I knew this was an animal making the noise, there was no woman or anyone else in the woods at this hour. We listened to the screams for a few more minutes and then suddenly, as abruptly as it began, it stopped. The smell began to dissipate and I knew whatever was out there at one time was now gone.

My faculties began to re-emerge and I realized our little dog slept on the porch. I ran to get her to make sure she was okay. When I went to the porch, I found her trembling and unnerved. She was cowering in the corner behind a potted plant. I knew immediately the dog was terrorized and it also heard the same as we did.

I scooped up our dog and brought her inside. When I picked her up, I could tell that whatever the odor was had attached itself to our poor puppy. Quickly I took her over to the sink and started to give her a fast bath. Whatever that smell was, was rancid and I did not want it in the house.

We did not mention it to our friends and after a few weeks, it was completely forgotten. Summer turned into winter and soon the holidays were upon us. One night we had a small dinner party. It was close to midnight and we were all standing on our front porch with our friends. We were saying farewell and wishing each other a happy new year. It had just snowed that evening, so everything was beautiful and peaceful. And then, from the nearby hillside, the screams returned once again.

Out of nowhere, the screams echoed and seemed to bounce off the fresh snow. our friends were terrified, not knowing what it was. Suddenly my wife and I remembered the events from this summer. It sounded like the screams were coming from the woods, and we all turned to look in that direction. It was extremely dark out that night, but there was a full moon. I could see shadows, but not clearly. One of our friends claimed to have seen something large walking on the road near the edge of the woods. Her eyes were much better than mine apparently. all I saw were Shadows that swayed back and forth. She described a figure that she said she could see clearly.

She described it as a large bear-shaped figure, but it was walking on two very long legs like a human. She said it was at lcast 8 feet tall and had extremely long arms. The figure appeared to her in a silhouette form, mainly due to the darkness, but she claimed to have been able to see the silhouette clearly. There was one more human scream, and our friends were startled beyond belief and headed to their car. Martha and I quickly went back inside, but this time we left our exterior lights on.

When morning arrived, I was curious to walk

outside to see what was out there. It had snowed the night before, so there was a fresh blanket of snow lying across our yard and the road. I walked over to the direction where I heard the screams the previous night. As I got closer, I began to see a strange set of tracks in the fresh snow. I had never seen tracks like these before. They resembled massive, human-like footprints. Each print measured a staggering eighteen inches in length, an eerie testament to the entity that haunted our nights.

The creek near our house had always been a place where I would go for a little peace and quiet. After those two events, I started hearing the unmistakable snap of branches breaking in the distance. I couldn't shake the feeling that I was no longer alone. I felt like something was in the woods and watched my every move. whatever was in the woods always remained just beyond my perception.

Chapter 10
UNKNOWN ENTITY

I'M A FIFTY-EIGHT-YEAR-OLD WEDDING PHOTOGRAPHER, so not someone who is prone to having paranormal experiences, especially not in the context of the work that I do. I've been doing this for thirty years now and have built a great name for myself, becoming one of the best photographers in the area and I do more than just weddings, but those are what I do most and what I've been told I do best. I sometimes must go to out of the way places to accommodate my clients and especially when it comes to the reception, I have found myself in the middle of nowhere on more than one occasion. That's what I was doing when I had my strange encounter. I still have no idea what I saw or came across that night but it's haunted me ever since. I don't do a lot of research as I am someone who believes the more you investigate the abyss, the more the abyss looks back at you. I love my life and what I do for a living but ever since that night I've been reluctant to go to receptions that take place in the woods without having at least one other person with me. Luckily I now have a few students who are more than happy to spend time at someone else's wedding reception and who love to do the grunt work that I no longer enjoy. That is, I don't tell them anything about what happened to me and the reason I give them for why they need to come with me is simple, I tell them it's to gain experience. That's the background on me, now let's get into my encounter.

I always do the photography at my friend's and family's weddings and receptions and throughout the years they've all brought me in more business with their friends and others they know. I did a wedding in the beginning of my career for a friend of a friend and about ten years ago the bride's daughter from that wedding was getting married and I was invited to be her photographer as well. The man she was marrying had a ton of money and everything she wanted, he made sure she got it. The budget for the wedding was more money than I will ever see in my life, let alone have the luxury of spending on one party, but they were a lovely couple and he was a nice guy. The wedding was held on the beach and was the usual, with not too many strange requests having been made or anything like that. The reception was something like I've never seen before though. It was being held on several acres of land with ten cabins on that land, and with a bunch of it cleared out, and with it being surrounded by a forest that everyone knows is haunted. Well, everyone but me because until I had my encounter I didn't believe in things like ghosts or anything like that. I'll say now though that I don't know what I saw, and that it could have been two very separate things. But anyway, I didn't believe it and thought it was funny when we finally all trekked out there and the bride's mother wouldn't stop crossing herself and spraying weird smelling spray all over the perimeter of the reception area. She said she was keeping the evil that dwelt in the woods away from the property and the wedding. The groom owned the land and the cabins and though I don't know what he used them for, he could have made his fortune just renting them out because it was gorgeous out there. The way they had set everything up was incredible and I still think about how wonderful that reception was. There was so much food, great music, and tons of people, with a select few who would be staying in the cabins that night. The groom walked me through his and the bride's cabin and it was like something out of the movies. We had a great time and I ended up getting a lot of spectacular photos, some of which are still in my portfolio today.

There was something that I couldn't quite put my finger on about the area though. It was like there was an overwhelming sense of doom and dread that kept coming over me as I walked around, trying to do my job. There were a few times when I looked through the lens of my brand new and state of the art cameras to try and get a shot of some of the guests and in the background I would see a blurred black mass that throughout shots seemed to be slowly moving around the perimeter the bride's mother had set up with her weird sprays. I wasn't the only one who felt it and the bride's mother spent most of the reception inside and refused to take any pictures outside at all once the sun went down, which was quickly after we got there. I would see the blurry masses in the lens but then when I would check the photo they wouldn't be there anymore so I thought maybe it was just something happening with the lighting or my being exhausted. The night went well, they paid me and I left. They were so sweet and offered me a room in one of the cabins so I didn't have to drive all the way home in the dark. This place was far out in the middle of nowhere but I couldn't be unprofessional, even though I knew them, and for as much as I had wanted to stay I decided it would be the best thing if I left. I said my goodbyes and took off. There was one road out of the complex and it was one I had to drive for almost a whole hour before I would reach the highway which would take me right home within twenty minutes or so. The road wasn't lit at all and the moonlight and my headlights were the only illumination I had to work with. That was somewhat usual for the area where all of this had happened though and so it wasn't anything I wasn't at least somewhat used to. I couldn't stop thinking about the masses I saw in so many of the photos and every time I thought about it I would get more and more scared. I got into my car and said goodnight to the father of the bride, before pulling out of the complex and exiting onto the dark road, surrounded only by thick forest on both sides. For the first twenty minutes everything was fine.

However, I was paying attention to the road but looked at the radio for a split second so that I could spin the dial and try to find a station that came in so I had something to listen to and didn't have to drive that already eerie road in complete silence. When I looked up something ran across the road. It looked like the blurry black mass I had seen in the pictures and I slammed on my brakes. In the seconds it took me to register something running in front of my vehicle and slam on my brakes, it was gone. It had disappeared into the woods on the right side. I looked around as I sat there and despite every instinct inside of me screaming for me to keep going and never look back, I was over-whelmed with the urge to move my car over to the side and get out. I was being literally compelled to follow whatever it was, though I didn't understand what was happening at the time. I pulled the car over, got out, locked the doors, and walked confidently into the woods in search of whatever had just run across the road. I had convinced myself it only looked like a blurry shadow and that it was small enough to have been a child or something. I don't know what I was thinking and as you can see the confusion is still very much with me. I had a small flashlight in my trunk for emergencies and I grabbed that as well before I started walking aimlessly into the darkened, allegedly haunted forest. I yelled to whatever it was but of course received no answer and I just kept on going. I shined the flash-light all around, trying to spot any movement but I didn't see anything. Suddenly it was like a lightbulb came on inside of my head and I realized what I was doing. Just as I turned around to go back to my car I heard some strange noises and a chill ran through my body as I recognized immediately what it was that I was hearing. I could still hear the crickets, owls, amphibians from the swamps and other nighttime creatures but it was like they were dulled somehow. The very careful and sneaky sounding sloshing of wet footsteps invaded my ears and I knew something was out there with me. Something was out there with me that was intelligent enough to try and creep up on me and that was soaking wet, probably having come from the swamp as it walked around where I was standing. "Splash, drip, drip, splash" it sounded like whatever it was had fins for feet or something and it sounded huge. Suddenly there was such a racket that my heart sank into my chest as I thought a stampede of wild hogs was coming towards me but even as the noise got closer and closer and as I kept the flashlight aimed right at where it was coming from, nothing ever appeared.

As soon as the stampede sounds started all the other noises I had been hearing, the normal ones, suddenly stopped and everything was silent except for the stampede noises coming straight at me. I saw a large black mass zigzagging through the trees and it was coming at me so fast it almost looked like a tornado for a moment. I turned and ran back to my car as fast as I could. As I was unlocking my door manually because my lock fob didn't work, I heard an extremely loud growling noise followed by the strangest noise of all, which was a loud hissing sound that sounded just like a snake would sound if it were an anaconda. The hissing was backed up by tremendous strength and the ground rattled with the voracity of it. I was shaking so badly that of course I dropped my keys in the dirt and immediately bent down to pick them up. I put them in the door and turned the lock before standing all the way up and getting in. I locked eyes with something else's eyes. They were huge and bright yellow, standing at around twelve feet up from the ground. I heard gentle and softer hissing then and it was coming right from where the eyes were. There was something out there and whatever it was, I didn't want any part of it. I got in my car and started the engine. As I drove off I looked in my rearview mirror and saw a large, blurry black mass quickly shoot back across the road to the other side where it had originally come from. I slammed on the gas pedal and didn't stop speeding out of there until I absolutely had to when I got onto the highway. I was paranoid for weeks that whatever it was had followed me. I don't know if I was dealing with a ghost, a demonic entity, an extraterrestrial species of something like a reptilian, all the above or something else altogether and honestly, as I said earlier, I don't want to know. I bring a student with me to all the receptions I attend at night and I haven't had to go back to that area ever since. Nothing bad happened to the bride or groom or any of the guests but now, instead of just rumors of the forest itself being haunted, I hear they're having a hard time with the luxurious cabin rentals business because they're allegedly haunted as well, with two of them not being able to keep guests there at all. They tend to run out in the middle of the night, or so I saw on a review of the place. I don't have anything else to say except I did have some very vivid nightmares immediately following the experience but nothing ever happened in the real world to me that seemed to be related and luckily nothing from that night attached itself to me, probably preferring to be inside of its real home, that haunted forest and those cabins, instead.

Chapter 11
BIGFOOT

IT WAS RATHER chilly in November of 2014. I was living in Raleigh, North Carolina, just on the outskirts of town. I moved to this location next to the forest and the river because I wanted to get close to nature, but I knew there'd always be a commute to "city life". One night I met a few friends in Raleigh for dinner and I was coming back home. It was around 10:30 PM.

When I pulled into my driveway, the headlights of my car spread out across the yard. They would light up the side of the brush and the woods to the left of my house. When I pulled in with my bright lights on, it always made animals scurry back away from the edge of the trees. they would go back into the woods where they belonged. They never really bothered me.

That night, as I stepped out of my car and started

towards the door, I heard a very bizarre noise in the trees. It sounded like a strange, guttural sound mixed with a chipmunk. I could tell it was coming from deeper within the woods. It was a sound I could not quite place. It was a mixture of anger and distress. My first thought was that my headlights were on bright and when I pulled in I agitated some nocturnal creature. But this was different. The intensity of the sound was unlike anything I had ever heard before.

I got out of my car and stood there for a moment, not closing the door. I did not want to make any noise and scare away the animal. I wanted to see what would happen. There was a chitter type of sound. I could tell there was a creature not too far from my house making that sound. About 50 yards away and deeper into the woods, there was another creature that was answering.

I closed the car door and secured the alarm. I walked a few steps and listened. I could still hear the chirping and chattering in the woods. I walked up on the steps of my porch to listen just a little bit more. I could hear something that sounded like wood knockings mixed in with the conversation. It sounded like a large tree limb was being hit against the side of a tree. There was a very distinct rhythm to the knocking. I stood with my hand on the doorknob, torn between wanting to go inside and the curiosity that was gnawing at me. I listened for about another 20 seconds and then went inside. The night was getting cold.

As I started to go to bed, I decided to crack my bathroom window a little for some fresh air. When I did I could hear something that sounded like grunts in the woods. Something closer to my house, maybe 40 yards away, was grunting at another creature in the woods. The vocabulary seemed to become more expansive and included grunts, wood knocks, and something that sounded like a person saying, "whoop whoop". This was a symphony of the woods I had never heard before. I turned off the lights, crawled into bed, and fell asleep being serenaded by the forest.

Later that night, I was jolted awake by a scream. I sat up straight in my bed, disoriented and trying to figure out what I was hearing. I looked at my clock. It was 5 AM. I had one more hour to sleep before I had to go to work. I tried to lay back down and go back to sleep, but for the next 30 minutes or so, I kept hearing the wild sounds in the woods.

These sounds seemed to originate from the same area in the woods where I heard the noises earlier in the evening. There were two creatures, their voices were mixed in the night, and they were having a conversation. It was just in a language I could not understand.

I listened for about 30 minutes. One would shout out and within a few seconds, the other would answer. I was slightly afraid but I was more curious. I wanted to know what was making the sounds in the woods.

I slipped out of bed, my footsteps muffled by the plush carpet, and cautiously made my way outside. It was still the middle of the night, as far as I was concerned, and it was dark everywhere. I could not see in front of me. There were no stars out and the moon was obscured. I could still hear the sounds in the woods, so I knew the creatures were still out there.

I stepped around to the side of my garage. I found myself standing in pure darkness. It was cold and I was shivering. I could have been shivering from fright or it could have been shivering from the night. I was not sure. I strained my ears to catch every detail that was spoken in the woods. I closed my eyes and strained to hear, and I picked up a very strange and unusual smell that was coming from the woods. It was coming from the direction of the first creature, but it was a faint smell of something rancid. It almost smelled like one of the stink bombs we would set off as kids during the 4th of July. It was a mixture of sulfur, lemon, and rotting dairy products that had been sitting in the sun for a day. It was a smell you don't forget, and when you encounter it later in life you are instantly taken back to that moment. I began to wonder, if I were ever to smell that again would I be taken back to this moment?

The strange sounds were like chattering. One creature, hidden in the depths of the forest, would speak, and about 50 yards away, another would respond in kind. Interwoven with the eerie chatter was a rhythm of wood knocking again. The knocks had a distinct pattern, a strange one that heightened the unrest within me.

I stood there in the dark for what felt like an eternity, unable to tear myself away. I was amazed at what I was hearing and wondered if others had heard such communications. I did not have neighbors close by, so it could have been that I was the only one to have ever heard this before.

When I jumped up from bed, my movements were an automatic response, like I was on autopilot. I grabbed my glasses and threw them on my face, grabbed my phone and put it in my pocket, and slipped on my shoes so I could run out the door. I had not even thought about it but the cell phone, now forgotten in my pocket, brought me back to reality when the alarm blared through the pocket of my pants.

In an instant, the sounds of the woods stopped. Silence descended like a heavy curtain and left me in the dark. I couldn't shake the feeling that whatever had been lurking in the woods was keenly aware of my presence. I knew I was filled with fear. I was not sure if they were going to race towards me or run away. Either decision made on their part slightly terrified me.

I never heard sounds in the woods like that again. I casually asked around over the next few weeks and my neighbors had never heard anything like that either.

Chapter 12
FOREST SPIRIT

I HAD JUST MOVED into my new house on a couple of acres of land and was in my own little heaven. Life hadn't been easy for me and I was forty years old before I was able to have a home that I had bought myself and with my own money. It was a dream come true for me, a little country cottage in the woods, where I could live my life away from other people and only see my neighbors when I felt like it. Even though I only had a couple of acres, all the houses in the development I moved into were separated by very high hedges and everyone seemed to keep to themselves. No one was unfriendly, just they seemed to be like me and enjoyed their privacy. It was about two months after I moved in that I saw the first of many strange creatures in my yard and I've seen dozens since, often they're coming into my yard from the woods. I grew up somewhat near where I bought the house and remember everyone saying that forest was haunted and had been for as long as the land had been settled and probably longer. As a kid I believed it but I had walked through parts of it on my way from one place to another a few times and aside from the feelings of being watched and like several sets of eyes were always on me, I had seen anything out there. I never thought about paranormal or supernatural experiences one way or another but when I did, like when someone else was discussing some sort of paranormal event or supernatural phenomenon, I always welcomed the idea of having some sort of interaction with some-thing not from here. Spring was turning into summer and I had an above ground pool in the yard that I was going to open so that when the warm weather came I would be ready. I had always been a water bug but lakes and the ocean freaked me out because I couldn't see the bottom and didn't like how my feet felt when it touched whatever was under there. It had always been my dream to have my own pool. I decided to eat a picnic lunch at a table I had placed in my yard not too far from the pool and the day was going very well for me, with the weather being lovely and the sounds of nature all around me lulling me into a false sense of security, despite my not knowing it was false at the time.

I was almost done cleaning the pool when suddenly I felt like someone was watching me from the woods. I suddenly got chills all up and down my spine despite it being a very warm day and I remember I shivered. I looked all around but didn't see anything. Despite it being broad daylight outside I felt very uncomfortable and for some reason, very scared as well. There was no one around either because no one was there with me, no one would be just randomly crossing or passing through that part of the forest as I had done when I was a kid because it was private property in that area and I had seen my neighbor drive off earlier that day. It was eerie but I decided to just put some music on to try and distract myself as I sat there and ate, trying to brush off the extreme feelings I was having that there was something out there that had set its sights on me. It worked for a little while, until I heard a very loud sound that was like a cross between a hawk and a pig, if you can imagine such a sound. It was incredibly loud and I knew it wasn't coming from any of the usual animals that were or that should have been out there at that time. Then, as I walked over to the table to turn the radio down, the strangest thing happened. It sounded like a mini stampede coming towards me. I instantly looked up to see about a dozen deer in my backyard. Three were doe, buck, and fawns alike and they were all staring back into the forest, not even seeming to realize or care that I was there. I watched in awe as they made noises like something was wrong and almost as though they were talking to one another. The loud and terrifying sound ripped through the air again and with it they all took off to the opposite side of my yard but were still within my sight and still not seeming to care that they were in such proximity to a human being.

I couldn't imagine what would make so many deer come out of the woods all at once or what would have been making them otherwise act so strangely. I walked right past them and none of them moved. All of them were still staring in the direction from which they had come into the yard, which was also the direction from which the strange sounds were coming. I walked over to the treeline but didn't see anything and suddenly another, very large buck, came running into my yard. It ran right past me without even looking at me and towards the other deer. They all started braying and took off, seemingly terrified of this very large buck. I laughed because it seemed like they were just scared off because of how large the buck was and I thought it was silly to think that deer could be being bullied. I turned around and went back to sitting at the table, eating, and listening to my music. The large buck stayed in my yard and was staring at me, which was starting to get very creepy. It had been a weird day as it was and so I decided that I was going to bring my food inside, clean up a bit in there and then go back out to finish the pool once the buck was gone. I know it sounds crazy but I didn't like the way it was looking at me. The moment I stood up to start gathering my things I heard the loud and terrifying hawk/pig noise again and I froze because it was coming from right where the buck had been standing. It was not a noise a buck or deer made, I was sure of that and knew it without a doubt. I slowly turned towards it and as I did I almost puked. I was so filled with dread and terror. My skin was absolutely crawling and sure enough, something strange was happening with the animal. It was glistening in the sunlight unlike anything I had ever seen before. It was like the air around it had taken on a shimmer and started glimmering. I could do nothing but stare at it because I was frozen with fear at the time. In the blink of an eye and with an extra crackle of shimmer around it, it began to transform.

It was no longer just a buck. It was standing on its two hind legs and the top of it was an incredibly muscular man. It wasn't like someone who had been taking steroids or over lifting at the gym. It was more than that and it was like it was filled with power. It was gorgeous. It had a human face with intense, very dark red eyes and long black hair. A crown of leaves went around its forehead, around the giant antlers that still framed its beautiful face. Its ears were pointed like an elves would be in fairytales and it had full and pouty, dark pink lips. It had sweat glistening down its body and for a moment I forgot that the bottom half of this Adonis was still a deer and how he had come to be in my yard in the first place. It just stood there for a moment, knowing fully well that I was admiring his physique and he stared off into the woods as I did so. Then it turned its head and I was instantly snapped out of my reverie. Its eyes were suddenly black again but not empty and fearful like most deer. They were evil and soulless and the smirk on its face was enough to turn my previously overheated blood cold. I tried to run but still couldn't move and my knees felt weak and as though I were about to faint just from the effort of trying to put one foot in front of the other. Just as suddenly as he had transformed he ran off into the woods at an abnormally fast rate of speed for either a man or a deer and was gone just as quickly as he had appeared as well. I was suddenly able to move, think and breathe again and I bolted for my door. I went inside and made sure everything was locked up tight. I drew all the shades and just sat there, terrified, and not knowing what to do next for more than an hour. I couldn't go back outside but I didn't know what else to do so I just continued to sit there. I looked it up and the closest thing that I can find to what I saw is a forest spirit. They're said to roam around forests all over the world and some of them are very helpful to humans and some of them not so much. Some of them, in fact, desire our blood and once I read that I decided to put the research away for a while. For the rest of the summer, I tried to put it out of my mind but on at least four occasions, one of which I had some of my family over for a visit, I would notice that suddenly everyone was inadvertently and without realizing it staying far away from one side of the forest or another. Then, a dozen or more deer of all different types would come running into the yard and nervously stand among us humans. Most of my guests found it fascinating but one time one of my teenage cousins came up to me afterwards and said she had seen a man in the woods who was half man and half deer. She hadn't mentioned it to anyone else for fear they would make fun of her or think she was using drugs or something. The only reason she said she told me was because she felt an obligation to do so, knowing in her heart that the gorgeous man/deer was evil incarnate and wanted to harm me. I pretended she must have gotten too much sun but I think she knew that I was full of it and didn't want to talk about it anymore.

It still happens, from time to time, and it's happened enough that I don't even go into the woods to pick berries or hike anymore. That's a bummer because those were some of the things I wanted to do that had endeared me to that house in the first place. It always starts the same exact way, with the feelings like someone is watching you. Then, the regular deer will come into the yard, almost stampeding one another and anything in their path to get away from whatever it is they're running away from. Then, the hideous and horrible, bone chilling hawk/pig noises, and then the forest spirit in the form of a beautiful man whose bottom half is that of a buck. I don't know what to make of it and ignore it as best as I can. I am reluctant to allow my younger family members to play in my yard alone and without supervision because I worry they'll wander off and be at the mercy of whatever that thing is that seems to have its sights set on me. Maybe they'll run into something much worse. Other than that, I've found some things online that I can do to keep it at bay and away from my property and I've tried some of them. Some have worked, albeit briefly, to keep it at bay and others didn't work at all. I don't know what to make of it and have somewhat come to terms with the fact that the woods belong to it and this house and my two acres belongs to me and so far, despite how evil it seems and that I know it is, it hasn't tried to hurt me or anyone else and so I'm content to live and let live. Maybe I'm crazy but there's more than just that thing I'm dealing with on my property and in my house and so I really try to not think of any of it so I don't drive myself crazy in the process. Thanks for letting me share this.

Chapter 13
HELLHOUND

IN THE EARLY 2000S, I decided to take my young son, Lucas, on a camping trip in the Sierra Nevadas, a place not too far from our home in Northern California. Lucas, just having turned six, was brimming with excitement. Ever since he could remember, I'd share tales of my childhood escapades amidst nature with my own father, and he was eager to have his own stories to tell.

Our home was nestled on the edge of a forest, a playground where we often embarked on little adventures – hiking, fishing, or just enjoying the beauty around us. However, this was going to be Lucas' first proper camping trip, a milestone, a rite of passage of sorts.

The day arrived, and as we made our way to the

campsite, Lucas was a bubbling pot of questions and stories. But, as we delved deeper into the forest, I noticed a shift in his energy. The excited chatter was replaced by a quiet observation. I figured it was the overwhelming vastness of the woods, which, for a little boy, could be a bit intimidating.

By evening, we reached a picturesque clearing which was to be our campsite. Surprisingly, despite it being the height of summer vacation for schools in the vicinity, there weren't many campers around.

We set up our tents – an extra one for Lucas, just in case he wanted his own space. He was eager, wanting to prove he was big enough for his own tent. Yet, as night fell, an eerie feeling began to envelop our camp. Lucas seemed distant, his cheerful demeanor clouded with a hint of unease. I asked him if he was alright, and he shrugged it off, saying he was just tired.

That night, after a delightful session of storytelling and marshmallow roasting, Lucas retired to his tent. I lay awake, the mysterious aura of the forest keeping me restless. In the dead silence, I began hearing whispers. It sounded like Lucas, but he wasn't alone. There was another voice, deep and unnatural.

Panicking, I tried to move, but an overwhelming lethargy held me down. My tent seemed to be surrounded by shadows, moving frenziedly, clouding my vision. Fighting every ounce of fatigue, I finally burst out to find Lucas walking trance-like towards the woods.

In the dim moonlight, an enormous shadow loomed. What emerged from behind a tree was something out of nightmares – a colossal, dog-like creature, its eyes ablaze, looking down at Lucas.

I screamed out, trying to break whatever hold it had on my son. Lucas, with a jolt, looked at me, tears streaming down, and ran into my arms. I quickly moved him into my tent, while the creature, now standing upright, growled menacingly.

It was nothing like I'd ever seen – almost a demonic fusion of man and beast. I remembered the prayers my grandmother taught me, and I started chanting them loudly, hoping to repel this entity. To my amazement, the creature shrieked in what sounded like pain. It morphed into a dark shadow and sped off into the woods, followed by the other shadows.

The next day, still shaken, we packed up and left. Lucas had no recollection of the night's events. He was puzzled by our abrupt departure, but I brushed it off, not wanting to expose him to the terror we had faced.

Curiosity drove me to research what we had encountered. From old regional myths and library archives, I deduced it was a hellhound, a guardian of the supernatural, often seen as an omen. But why it was interested in Lucas remained an unsettling mystery.

Years have passed. Lucas is now in college, a strong, adventurous young man, often reminiscing about our camping trips, thankfully with no memory of that horrifying night. But for me, every rustle in the woods, every shadow brings back memories of that night, reminding me of the mysteries the world holds.

Chapter 14
FOREST DEMON

MY UNSETTLING ENCOUNTER happened in 1995 when I was merely sixteen and residing in the southern regions of Canada with my aunt and uncle. They owned a sprawling ranch, and due to my parents being rather aloof, I proposed moving in with my elderly relatives to assist them. Soon after, I relocated from Nova Scotia to this secluded southern village. The village's populace barely numbered a hundred, so I've refrained from naming it to dissuade any curious adventurers from seeking out the terror I faced.

The high point of my time there was the horses my relatives kept. One, in particular, felt like my very own. Under my aunt and uncle's supervision, life was serene until the summer when my life took a terrifying turn.

That summer, my parents decided to visit. The

reunion, filled with relatives, looked promising. One evening, to vent some steam after a heated conversation with my parents, I took my trusted horse into the nearby forest. The path was familiar; however, this night would be unlike any other.

As we ventured deeper, my horse became unsettled. Searching for the cause, my eyes landed on what seemed to be a deer. Yet, upon closer inspection, this was no ordinary deer. Standing on its hind legs, it combined a deer's features with a humanoid physique. Its eyes burned fiercely red and conveyed pure malevolence. A chilling realization swept over me - this was no mere forest creature, but an ancient forest demon.

In sheer terror, I urged my horse to race back to the ranch. The demonic entity pursued us, its grotesque form bounding eerily close. But as soon as we reached the safety of the ranch, it vanished.

I rushed to confide in my uncle, who revealed his own past encounters with this entity. He believed I had faced a malevolent forest spirit. Sleep evaded me that night and many after, as the demon's eyes seemed to peer at me from the forest's edge. My beloved horse fell sick mysteriously and passed away three weeks later. My uncle believed the demon played a part in its demise. While grateful for my own safety, the trauma remains imprinted on my soul.

After that terrifying night, life on the ranch was forever altered. I tried to re-establish some semblance of normalcy, but the woods' edge, which once seemed inviting and calm, now held an air of foreboding. The once soothing songs of the crickets now seemed to carry a sinister undertone, and the trees appeared to cast longer, more ominous shadows.

My uncle, seeing my distress, decided to share more about the history of the demon, hoping knowledge would help combat my fear. It was said that centuries ago, this part of Canada was inhabited by indigenous tribes who worshipped various spirits of nature. While most of these spirits were benevolent, a few were malevolent and sought to harm rather than help. The demon I had encountered was named "Wanageeska," meaning "Ghost Deer" in the local tribal language.

Wanageeska was a guardian spirit gone rogue. He once protected the forest and its inhabitants but was corrupted by a dark shaman's rituals, transforming him into a creature of malevolence. Those who ventured too deep into his territory after dark were said to never return.

My uncle admitted that when they had bought the ranch, the local tribes had warned them about the forest's dark spirit. He had brushed off these warnings as mere superstitions. Over the years, however, he had several encounters with Wanageeska, each time narrowly escaping its grasp.

Wanting to protect the ranch and its inhabitants, my aunt, uncle, and I decided to seek help. We consulted a tribal elder, a woman named Nuna, known for her vast knowledge of ancient rituals and spirits.

Nuna, after listening to our tale, agreed to perform a cleansing ceremony to ward off Wanageeska. She explained that while we couldn't destroy the demon, we could create boundaries that it wouldn't cross. However, she also warned us that the ceremony would challenge our spirits and test our resolve.

The night of the ceremony was moonless, making the forest appear even more menacing. Nuna created a large circle in the ranch's clearing, using various herbs, stones, and tribal symbols. As she chanted, the wind seemed to pick up, and a thick fog enveloped the area.

Suddenly, out of the thick fog, the familiar red eyes of Wanageeska appeared. It seemed to challenge Nuna, but she remained steadfast, her voice rising in defiance. After what felt like hours, a brilliant white light emanated from the center of the circle, and with a deafening roar, the demon retreated back into the forest.

The fog lifted, and the ranch was bathed in the soft glow of dawn. Exhausted but relieved, we thanked

Nuna, who left us with a warning to always respect the forest's boundaries and never venture into Wanageeska's territory after dark.

Life on the ranch slowly returned to its peaceful rhythm. While the memory of that terrifying encounter never truly faded, the knowledge that we had taken steps to protect ourselves brought some comfort. The forest edge, though still a reminder of the lurking danger, also became a testament to our resilience and the age-old battle between light and darkness.

Chapter 15

GOATMAN

IT WAS a hot and humid night, typical for a Texas summer. Much of what's always like this time of year. I slowly drove my old pickup truck down the dark road leading to the Alton bridge, like I did every year on this day. July 18th - Ben's birthday. Had he not taken his own life he would have been 32 years old today. My cousin was more like a brother to me. My best friend took his own life on this bridge ten years ago.

Now, before you judge me for the story, I'm about to tell you that you should know that I've never been the superstitious type. That why I came down here. It's just old wood and metal keeping this thing functioning. I half wonder why Ben would've ever have chosen a place like this to end it all. You see, some folks say this bridge is haunted by a creature called the goat man.

Stories of a half-man, half-goat who attacks people on the bridge at night. I've never even had a blink of a problem, so I never put much stock in those legends...never had any trouble in all the times I came here to remember Ben.

But something felt different this year. Maybe it was just getting older, but the night seemed darker, the silence heavier. I parked the truck and stepped out, grabbing the bottle of whiskey from the passenger seat - Ben's favorite brand. The bridge looked Pitch black ahead of me. I took a deep breath and started walking, taking a swig from the bottle. The whiskey burned going down but warmed my chest. "Happy birthday, Ben," I said aloud. My voice echoed off the sides of the bridge. I walked halfway across and leaned on the railing, peering down at the water flowing below. It was here that Ben took his final breaths. I sighed, taking another sip. Wishing my cousin peace in the next life if there was one.

That's when I first heard it - a faint creak of footsteps from somewhere behind me on the bridge. I spun around, squinting into the darkness. Nothing there. Probably just an animal, I told myself. I wasn't afraid. Not of ghosts, not of legends. I turned back to the railing and lifted the bottle towards the moonlight. "Cheers, cuz." The footsteps creaked again, closer this time. I whipped my head around. "Hello?" I called out. Silence answered. Heart pounding, I shuffled backwards until I felt the railing against my back. The footsteps started again, slow, and heavy like boots on old wood. Closer they came, until they sounded just over my shoulder. I spun to the left and right, seeing nothing but shadows. "Who's there?" I shouted. My voice cracked. The footsteps stopped for a moment. I let out a shaky breath.

Just my mind playing tricks, I thought. I poured out a splash of whiskey into the water below. "Miss you, Ben." The footsteps scrambled toward me fast, like something running. Before I could react, I felt a rope loop around my neck and yank tight. I gasped for air as the noose cinched tighter, burning my throat. I flailed wildly, landing punches at the empty air. Some unseen force lifted me by the neck until just my toes scraped the wooden boards beneath me.

I clawed at the rope, but my fingers passed right through it, finding only my own skin. My vision started to darken. I swung my arms behind me, feeling nothing. Just as my strength faded, the tension on the rope released and I collapsed to the ground. Gulping the night air, I scrambled away on my hands and knees. At the end of the bridge, I turned back - still no one in sight. I pressed a hand to my bruised throat as my pulse pounded in my ears. After a few minutes, my breath slowed enough for me to stand and stumble to my truck.

I peeled out and sped down the road, not stopping until I was a mile away. Only then did I pull over and try to make sense of what happened. I sat there stunned, going over it again and again in my mind. There was no denying it - something attacked me on that bridge. And if it wasn't a person...could the goat man be real? I dug my old smartphone out of the glovebox and did some searching.

Story after story appeared, warning people to stay away from the old Alton bridge at night. Reports of a tall beast-like creature ambushing folks over the years. Descriptions of glowing red eyes and a twisted mix of human and goat features. Complaints to police about unexplained ropes or scratches appearing on anyone brave or foolish enough to lurk on the bridge after dark. My hands shook and my throat ached as I scrolled through image after image of the demonic creature folks had witnessed at the bridge.

No one could explain where the goat man came from or why it haunted that place. But there was no more denying the truth for me. Tonight, I had investigated its cold, inhuman eyes and felt its rage. I had escaped by the skin of my teeth. I tossed the phone onto the seat next to me. As the adrenaline wore off, grief returned. My cousin was gone. And now, it seemed, so was my yearly tradition of visiting that bridge on his birthday. As much as I wanted to honor Ben, I couldn't risk the goat man finding me again.

I reached over to rub the fading red mark on my neck and whispered "Sorry cuz, guess I'll have to remember you another way from now on. Ain't neither of us got no business with that devil." I started up the truck and took one last look down the empty road toward the bridge before driving off into the night, leaving Old Alton behind me.

Chapter 16
BIGFOOT

FOR YEARS, my buddies and I had been making our way to our favorite camping spot. It was in the middle of Kentucky, at the base of a mountain. There were several rolling hills and valleys in the area. Civilization was coming and the area was changing drastically. There was a lot of clear-cutting going on and new communities were being built. We tried to enjoy this area before it was destroyed. We had been on this trip for two days.

There was one incident when I decided to just walk around. My two friends, Billy and Tom, were fishing. I wasn't feeling too well so I was sleeping in my tent. When I started to feel better, I knew I needed to get up and move so I could totally shake the 24-hour bug. I really did not feel like hiking, but I went over to a trail that I knew. It had a fantastic View of the mountains. As I was walking over to the trail, I heard a very strange sound coming from the road nearby. I was curious and I walked over to see what was making the sound. There, on the side of the mountain, I saw a dark shadowy figure. This was one of the areas that had recently been clear-cut, and I had a clear line of sight of the extremely large figure on the mountain.

I stood there silently and watched for a few minutes. I did not move or say anything, so I was perfectly disguised next to a tree. Finally, the large creature turned around and saw me. When it did, it wasted no time at all running away and quickly disappeared Into the Woods that lay just beyond the clearing.

I brushed it all off, thinking that it was nothing more than my eyes playing a trick on me. I went back over to camp and by that time my friends were back with dinner for the night. They asked how I was feeling and I told him fine and what I had just seen. They both chuckled and laughed at me. They dismissed it and jokingly they said I must have seen Bigfoot.

That night as we were cooking dinner, there the most unsettling odor that drifted into our campsite. The stench was overwhelming. It reminded me of spoiled food left to rot in the sun. We scanned the vicinity, expecting to find a neighboring campsite with culinary misadventures. There were no signs of fellow campers nearby. The stench was getting very intense and my stomach was beginning to churn again. I thought I would go lay down in the tent for a few minutes to see if that would stop the queasiness.

After dinner, we sat around the fire, had a few beers, and were just talking. The nights were starting to get a little chilly, and I moved in a bit closer to the fire. Right when I did, something hit Billy in the back. We all started laughing when he jumped up and looked around and tried to find what hit him in the back. but before we could catch our breaths something hit me in the back as well. My earlier amusement quickly turned to slight anger. We started to look around at the ground around us. Pebbles lay scattered about, unmistakably thrown at us. It was apparent that someone - or something - had been aiming for us. The force that hit us in the back told me that it was something big and strong that had thrown it. I instantly wondered; had the creature I saw on the mountain started throwing rocks at us now?

Not to be outdone, Tommy, the only one amongst us who had not been struck, jumped up to his feet. He flailed his arms wildly, shouting at whatever lurked in the woods, demanding it to "cut it out".

There was an immediate response to Tommy from

the woods. We heard a strange sound. It was a bizarre vocalization coming from the middle of the woods. Every time Tommy shouted something, the creature in the woods would mimic the cadence of whatever Tommy shouted. Clearly, it was intelligent and it was trying to communicate.

Eventually, we managed to calm Tom down, convincing him to sit back down and have a beer. Our campsite had grown tense, we were on high alert and we watched the tree line to see if we could determine where our unseen tormentor lurked.

Whatever was in the woods had our full attention. I think that was its twisted plan the entire time. the onslaught of rocks being thrown had stopped. The air was still heavy though. That rotten smell was starting to drift back in too. We formed a circle around the campfire with our backs to the fire. We were all looking into the woods, hoping to find some sort of movement.

I could hear something very large moving in the trees. There were also the sounds of very large branches snapping. It sounded like something very large and heavy. It was running through the woods, breaking branches as it ran. The sounds of the breaking branches and the Twigs snapping were getting further and further away from us. It sounded like the creature was running back to wherever it came from.

I knew if that was a real predator, it was not going to give up so easily. I had a sinking feeling in my stomach. I immediately thought that something was trying to give us a false impression of it running off, While others of its kind stayed in the shadows and close to us. My instincts kicked in, and I went back into my tent and got my rifle.

I cocked the rifle like they do in the movies, making a very loud sound. I wanted whatever was in the woods to know that I was not afraid and I was in charge.

Startled by the noise, the forest fell eerily quiet. Whatever had been walking around us seemed to have second thoughts. The rest of the night passed without further incidents. Billy and Tommy decided to sleep by the fire and to keep it going all night. I, however, retreated to my tent.

The next morning, my friends and I decided to investigate the sounds of the evening. Tommy discovered large footprints that were near my tent. They were barefoot and huge. At one point, the footprints crossed over each other, as if something had made a sudden, abrupt movement and smudged the tracks in the process. The footprints were about 17 inches long, much longer than any of our feet. I know they were not there when we set up the tents a few days earlier.

Billy and Tom found a new sense of bravery with

the sunlight, and they decided to track the prints. they could only track them for a little bit. The footprints led into the woods and disappeared quickly.

As we stood on the edge of the woods, I noticed something. several large branches, most of them at a height of around 10 feet, were twisted and snapped off the sides of the trees. Something large had run through here and broke the branches. Oddly enough, there was no trace of the broken branches in the immediate vicinity. The breaks all looked fresh on the trees, so the limbs should be directly below the trees unless something carried them off.

After that, there were no more events that happened. That was our last trip before the entire area was clear-cut.

—

CONTINUE
THINGS IN THE WOODS: VOLUME 2

About the Author

Erik Lake, a pen name adopted to maintain privacy, is a seasoned author with a deeply-rooted passion for the mysteries of human culture and the unexplained. Prior to embarking on his writing career, he served as a professor of anthropology at a prestigious university, where he was celebrated for his captivating lectures and scholarly publications. His academic pursuits led him across the globe, from the jungles of the Amazon to the mountainous terrains of the Himalayas, in search of understanding the complexities of human behavior and tradition.

Throughout his academic tenure, Erik developed a keen interest in folklore, myths, and the stories that often go untold or are overshadowed by mainstream narratives. It was this curiosity that led him to explore themes of the paranormal and the enigmatic phenomena that challenge our understanding of reality.

Since leaving academia, Erik has devoted himself to full-time writing, specializing in works that merge his anthropological background with topics often considered too taboo or unsettling for conventional scholarly dialogue.

Erik Lake brings to the literary world a rare blend of academic rigor and open-minded curiosity. Whether he's shedding light on cryptids, spirits, or age-old legends, his works provide a well-balanced blend of skepticism and wonder, prompting readers to question their own beliefs and perspectives.

Away from the pen and paper, Erik enjoys hiking, amateur photography, and spending time with his family in a quaint, undisclosed location surrounded by nature's untamed beauty. Yet, the woods for him are not just a retreat but an ongoing field of research—a labyrinth of endless questions and bewildering phenomena that continue to fuel his prolific writing career.

Also by Free Reign Publishing